The Chicken

And

The Egg

By
Beatrice Ann

Eden House/ New York

Kenneth & Deffanie— without whom I would have remained un-hatched and unlearned. Thanks for giving everything.

The Chicken and the Egg were standing in line.
At the very same time, the two arrived.

**The Chicken and the Egg were of the same mind.
So the Chicken and the Egg stood side by side.**

The Chicken and the Egg didn't know what to do.
"You first," said the Chicken. "You're the younger of us two."

But the Egg started thinking, as eggs all want to do. "You first," said the Egg. "I'm not as old as you!"

"C'mon," said the Chicken.
"I've been there. I've done that."

"Ok," said the Egg. "Better reason for me to stand back.
You've got the *experience*. You've earned it in fact.
Everything you've ever done has led to this act."

"Oh Little Egg,
how little do
you know.

When you're as old
as I, you're in no
rush to go,"

Said the Chicken to
the Egg as he
wobbled to and fro.

"Go forth young one. Go forth. Go! Go!"

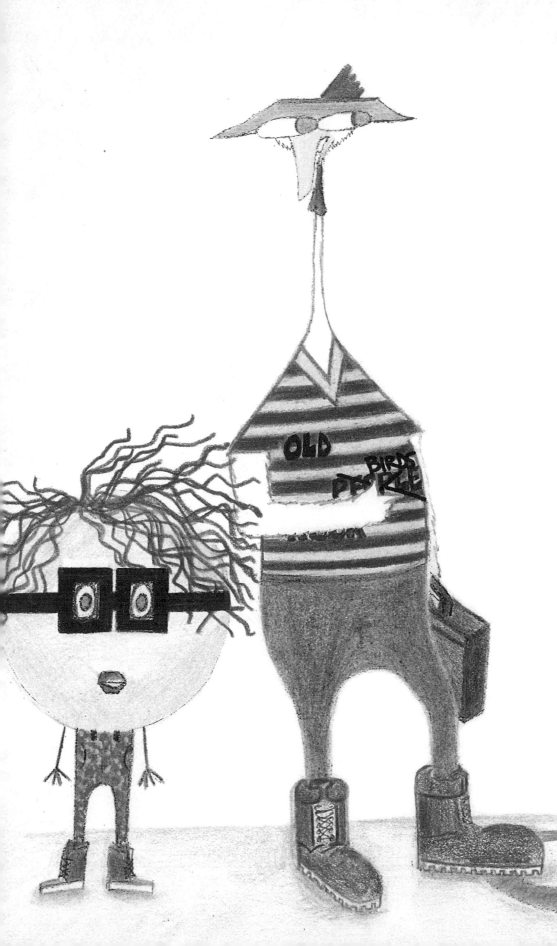

"I get it," said the Egg. "I'm young, but I'm not blind.
Believe me, you have been so much more than kind.
Which is why it's truly difficult I find,
To walk right up and leave you behind."

"Go!" yelled the Chicken.

"No," said the Egg.

hen I'll get on my knees and beg!"

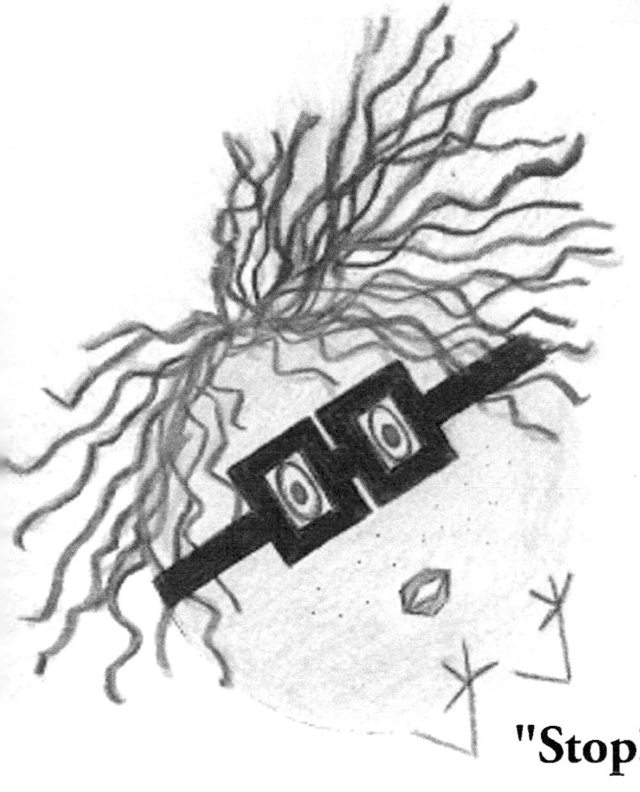

"Stop! You're going to hurt your leg!"

The Chicken and the Egg went head-to-head.

"Ahem," said the hand from the ticket line.
"When will you two make up your mind?
If you don't act now, you're wasting your time.

"We're so very sorry!" the Chicken and Egg cried.
"We somehow arrived here side by side.
We've done all we could. We really have tried."

"Who should go first?"

"Why don't you decide?"

Introducing...

Lizzie the Frill-necked Lizard

ANd...

Turbo the Shell-less Turtle

Draw a circle around the one that *you* think should go first. YOU DECIDE!

or Videos, T-Shirts, otes and More, Visit our Website.

WWW.THECHICKENANDTHEEGG.COM